Praise for

DEMENT

"With **DEMENT** Lyle Perez-Tinics sets you spiraling down a helter-skelter of madness where the mayhem increases with every turn. The thin line between reality and insanity blurs more with each new page. An unsettling, fast-paced nightmare."

- David Moody, author of the **AUTUMN** and **HATER** series

"Part zombie novel, part ghost story, part insane journey, Lyle Perez-Tinics' **DEMENT** is an engrossing tale of one man's struggle against the undead--and his strange destiny in the apocalypse."

- Craig DiLouie, author of **THE INFECTION** and **TOOTH AND NAIL**

"With **DEMENT**, Lyle Perez-Tinics intertwines a zombie story and a ghost story into a tight intense ride that will keep you guessing until the last exciting page."

- Jonathan Moon, author of **HEINOUS**

"Nightmare bleeds into reality in Lyle Perez-Tinics' demented new blend of splatterpunk and psychological horror."

- D.L. Snell, co-author of **PAVLOV'S DOGS**

Rainstorm Press
PO BOX 391038
Anza, Ca 92539
www.RainstormPress.com

ISBN 10 – 1-937758-25-7
ISBN 13 – 978-1-937758-25-7

Library of Congress Control Number: 2012911847

Dement
Publisher: Rainstorm Press
Copyright © 2012 by Rainstorm Press
Text Copyright © 2012 Lyle Perez-Tinics
All rights reserved.

Interior book design by –
The Mad Formatter
www.TheMadFormatter.com

Cover Design by: © April Guadiana

DEMENT

A Psychological Zombie Novella

By Lyle Perez-Tinics

Rainstorm Press

More Works by
Lyle Perez-Tinics

As Writer

Death's Too Short
Existing Dead
Rising from the Tempest
25 Ways to get Rid of a Zombie

As Editor

The Undead That Saved Christmas:
Vol. 1, 2 and Vampire Edition
Signals from the Void
Code Z: A Zombie Hospital Anthology

DEMENT

Chapter One

I take in a deep breath as I plan my next words. "The price of gold hasn't been doing well," I say, to the frail old woman across the counter. Her many years are clearly indicated by the wrinkles in her face. I hold the clasp of her 14-karat gold Figaro Link necklace between my index finger and thumb. The length of the necklace dangles in midair like a male hypnotist would his watch. I drop it into my cupped left hand and bounce it up and down. "And there isn't that much weight to it. The necklace is only 10-grams."

I'm lying. The scale placed its weight at 26.6-grams, but I can take this old woman. The scale sits on a table against the wall, craftily positioned, so that one's body blocks any customer's view of the numbers.

This old lady is the kind of customer pawnbrokers love. I can see in her face that she agrees with my assessment of her necklace's light weight. I can also see that she's desperate and might accept any lowball offer I give her.

She nods her head, as I continue to talk. I give her my 'I'm here to help you speech, so I can judge what her reaction will be when I give her an offer.

"... So, with that being said," I continue, as I place her necklace on the black vinyl pad between us. The florescent lights above make the gold twinkle as it is flawlessly cleaned. "I can offer you a fifty dollar loan for your necklace."

The old lady nods then asks, "And, how much for a pawn?"

There's that dreadful question again. When will customers understand that a loan is a pawn? I hate it when they ask me that.

"A loan is a pawn," I say, grinding my teeth in an attempt to conceal my anger.

"Oh ..." a quick embarrassed laugh leaves her mouth, and then she continues. "Well, how much can I get if I just sell it to you?" Her voice falls from a high-pitched squeal to a low hum. "I really need two hundred dollars." She stares into my face giving me a sad, pitiful look.

That doesn't work on me lady. I've heard it all, I think to myself.

"My step grandson has just passed, and I need to

come up with as much money as possible for his funeral costs."

I was wrong. That's one I've never heard. Now the real haggling starts. This lady is in no condition to be making financial decisions. I couldn't care less what's going on in her life. My job is to make money any way I can.

"Two hundred dollars?" I ask, with a skeptical look on my face. "That's a little steep for your chain." I pick the necklace back up and pretend to examine it, again.

In reality, this lady's request is feasible. I do the math in my head. This lady is entitled to at least $320.00, but of course I won't do it. It's my job to make as much money as possible for this store, and it's customers, in situations like this, who make my job easy.

"Well," I begin, as I set the necklace back down. "I can't do two hundred. The closest I can get is one hundred. If you were to sell it to me, that is." I look into her face and see that she's thinking about my offer. If she's considering settling for one hundred, then adding a bit more money to the pot should seal the deal.

"OK, how about this," I lower my voice, as I lean in closer. The elderly woman reeks of cinnamon and a musky scent, one that I can't quite put my finger on. "If you don't say anything to my bosses, I'll throw in an extra $25.00. So, if you're OK with $125.00, then we have a deal. Let's just hope I don't get in trouble for this."

I smile and tilt my head at the old lady as I lean back away from her. Her face betrays her delight. That's what I like to see. The customer now thinks I'm her friend, so I play along, knowing all the while that I've got her mental grip.

"I'll take it!" the lady says, filled with joy.

"Wonderful," I say, as I move over to the computer. "May I just have your ID?"

She hands me her card, and I type in all her information. Her name is Maggie Bliss, age 78, height 5'2", weight 105 lbs., eyes blue, and hair white.

"Y'know," I say, as I type, "my last name is, Bliss, as well. My first name is, Mark, but my friends call me, Marky-B. We have similar names."

I hit the print button. Maggie laughs as I walk to the printer to retrieve the contract. I wait a few seconds for the printer to stop. I rip on the dotted line and bring the detached contract back to the counter and place it in front of her.

I smile at her and take a pen out of my pants pocket. "I'll need you to sign on this red X," I point to the X using the pen, "and I'll need your thumbprint in this little box."

As she signs the paperwork, I slide the necklace into a small manila envelope. I staple a purchase ticket to the cover and check on Maggie.

"All done?" I ask. She nods as I take the contract and look it over. "OK, everything looks good. Now, I just need to get you some money." I constantly smile at the old lady, feeling no remorse for what I've done.

I stack the contract with the rest of the day's purchases, and then I head to the back room where I find a place in the safe for the necklace. I open the register and retrieve the money, then walk back into the showroom.

"And here we are," I say. "Fifty, one hundred, twenty, and five, makes one hundred twenty-five."

"Thank you so much, for the help," Maggie says with delight as she scoops up her money. "I will be telling all my friends about this place. They have all just been dying to find a place like this." She adds, with a tint of malevolence.

"Well, thank you," I reply, ignoring her sudden change in voice. "You have a wonderful day, now."

The old lady puts the money in her purse and smiles as she walks out the two shatterproof glass doors. The shop closes early on Saturdays, so she is my last customer. I love leaving work while the sun is still out.

As she steps onto the sidewalk, Maggie looks back and gives me one final smile.

"That's what I like to see," I mumble to myself as I close the glass doors. "I rip her off, and now, she's my friend."

Maggie looks to the west and begins walking up Scandon Avenue. I'm still trying to put the lock on the doors, when I hear a scream. I look out the windows to see the old lady being forced to the ground by a man twice her size. He has her pinned, both his arms holding her shoulders down. His head moves down to the side of her neck and snaps back violently. Blood drips down his mouth while he chews.

Chapter Two

"Holy shit!" I yell in shock and surprise. Quickly running to the safe, I grab the store's firearm. The Glock 17 is always loaded in case there's trouble. I may have just taken this lady for a ride, but I don't want to see her get hurt.

When I reach the front of the shop again, the man is still on top of Maggie. I hustle up the driveway and head west when I reach the street.

I stop only a few feet in front of the man. He pays no attention to me and continues biting at Maggie, eating her old wrinkled flesh. The scene is baffling.

"Stop!" I yell, "Get off of her!" I point the Glock directly at the man.

The man looks up at me. Streams of blood conjoin on the tip of his chin and drip down onto Maggie's dark blue sweater.

I stop for a second and look up and down the street. No one is around.

How long was I talking to Maggie in the store? I mentally ask myself.

Scandon is a very busy street. People are always strolling around, looking in the shops. But now everyone is gone. The only people on the street are Maggie, her attacker, and me. I snap out of my daze.

"Get the hell off of her right now!" I bark at the man, who continues to glare at me. It's as if the man can't comprehend what I'm saying or can't understand my actions.

His face is vacant, and his eyes are glazed over with what looks like clouds of white smoke. Blood continues to drip from his mouth. The man grinds his teeth and lifts his upper lip. I can see bits of flesh between the gaps of his grill. There's a stench of decay coming from somewhere in the area. As a gust of wind blows, I realize it's coming from him. The rotten smell, and the sight of him eating Maggie makes me gag, but I control my nausea.

Poor Maggie lies motionless beneath as he gives her one last look and then rises to his feet. He stretches his arms out toward me and slowly advances. I take a few steps back, still pointing the gun at him. I lay my index finger against the trigger and grip the pistol tightly.

"Stay the fuck back," I order. "Don't come any

closer!" The man shows no comprehension. His eyelids go as wide as possible as his mouth opens drops open and a poor, agonizing attempts to breathe leaves his throat. "Don't come any closer or I'll shoot!"

He's only a few feet away from me, now; I can't take any more chances. I'm sure the cops will understand that I had no choice but to put this guy down. Maybe one of the outside security cameras witnessed the entire event.

Stop thinking about it and just do it, I tell myself, and then squeeze the trigger.

The bullet hits the man dead center in his chest. He falls back, and I begin hyperventilating. The incident only lasts for a matter of seconds as the man hurls to the ground and lands, arms akimbo, to the hard concrete sidewalk. I glance at the mans face, his eyes are closed and his frame is motionless. The man is dead, and I killed him. I've never had to shoot anyone before. Adrenaline rushes through my veins, overwhelming me with excitement, with the feeling that this is something I've been craving. For a moment, I just revel in the rush.

I shake off my reverie, take my cell phone out of my pocket, and dial 9-1-1. As my thumb hovers over the green send button, I hear another moan from the ground. The man's eyes reopen revealing that glossy white smoke. He turns his head to glare at me and drags himself to his feet, again. My mouth drops, and my stomach feels hollow. I can't believe what I'm seeing.

"Holy shit!" Is the only thing I can yell, my voice echoes through the streets. I put my cell phone back in my pocket and raise the gun toward the man, again. I fire a few more shots, without thinking. I will empty the entire magazine on this person, if it stops them from advancing. On my third shot, the round punches through his forehead. As the bullet breaks through his skull, a look of disbelief comes over his face. The projectile does not exit the back of his head. I can picture the round ricocheting inside his skull and turning his brain into a pink soup. The man drops to the ground, lying still, beside Maggie.

I am hyperventilating, again. I can't get enough of this rush, so I stand over the man's body and fire a few more rounds into his head. His body jumps with each shot. I stand there, for a second, looking at Maggie and then, looking at the disfigured man I just killed. I realize that something had come over me, something I couldn't control. It felt like I was letting the real person -inside of me- out, and he was dangerous.

I hear footsteps behind me, slow and shuffling footsteps, a lot of them. I turn around to face at least ten more crazy people, covered in blood, all with the same vapid, dead look the cannibalistic man had worn. They stare at me with hungry white eyes; their jaws snapping open and shut with every step they take. Their legs don't appear to bend at the knees; it's as though they're stiff and struggling to walk. Suddenly, one of them moans. The sound vibrates my body with chills.

One of the females is missing an arm, blood and ligament oozes out of the wound. As she approaches me, I notice bite marks on her stub. A male bumps into a green car parked on the street. The alarm goes off sending a blaring beep into the sky. He doesn't seem to notice the vehicle is blocking his path. This scene would almost be comical, if I were in a movie. They continue to moan as they wobble toward me.

My first impulse is to run, but something inside me tells me to stand and fight. I have no idea what is going on, but I know something is terribly wrong. More freaks come out of a small taco shop, I'd assumed was deserted; two males and one female. They must be the workers; the two cooks, and the cashier. Two of them turn in my direction and glare vacantly. They wear blood stained clothes, and one of the male's face is completely disfigured, as if his head was dunked into a pot of hot cooking oil. Loose skin droops down his face, as he follows the more preserved freaks in front of him. Their eyes squint, in what I assume, is an attempt to determine who I am. They turn robotically and stagger toward me. Their mouths open in anticipation.

The noise from the alarm continues to ring out. I

look further down Scandon Ave and see more monsters shambling out of every corner possible. Maybe the noise from the car alarm is drawing them to this place.

The insane folks behind me are closing in on my position. I take a few steps back until I feel something tugging on my pants. I look down to find Maggie grabbing my left leg with her hands, as she slowly moves her head closer to my shin. Her mouth opens, and she gives out a loud hiss. When she does that, blood rushes out of an open gap on her neck. Her eyes are not like the others. They're not smoky white, but instead are a strange color red. I have never seen this color before, it's almost hypnotic. Looking at her eyes closely, I can't believe it's even a color in my visible spectrum.

I kick her off with my right leg and point the Glock at her head. I pull the trigger. The round enters the top of her head, ripping away half of her scalp. She continues moving, thrashing around like a crazed animal. I raise my left heel over her head and with as much strength as I can manage, I stomp down. There is an unexplainable sound and a squashing sensation, as though I've just stepped on a cantaloupe. Brain matter and blood cover my steel-toe work shoes. Maggie lies still, as one of her eyes pops from the disgorged socket and rolls on the ground.

The stench, and the gore turn my stomach to the point of no return. I vomit all over Maggie's body and all over my shoes and pants. I realize that the freaks and the demented people from the taco shop are inches behind me; my nausea gives way to a drive for self-preservation.

The arms of the insane claw for any hold they can find on my body. Their moans grow louder in anticipation. The way to Al's Hardware, a small hardware store on my left is clear, for the moment; so I head in that direction. I nearly trip over my own feet, as I push the demented away.

Chapter Three

I storm into Al's Hardware and slam the door shut behind me. I lean against the back of the door and try to catch my breath. My respite is short-lived, as a loud bang erupts from the other side of the door. I jump away, wheeling around to aim the Glock at the door. I stand there waiting for it to open, but it does not. Instead, more hands pound on the wooden, thick door accompanied by high-pitched moans that sound like cries for help. I can see the demented through the large glass window behind the cashier counter. They don't notice me; their focus is riveted on the door.

I hear a footstep from within the store. I look behind me and see a human figure emerging from the shadows.

"Hello?" I ask, my voice cracking.

A loud, drawn-out moan is the only response. Without hesitation, I point the barrel of the Glock at the figure's head. My finger wraps around the trigger, and I squeeze.

Click.

That's the worst sound in the world. The gun is empty. In all the commotion, I didn't notice when the slide clicked back. I have no more rounds on me; I'm not even sure we have any back at the shop.

"Fuck," I mutter under my breath.

I holster the firearm on my belt. The figure continues to stagger toward me in that unnerving robotic manner. I look nervously around for something with which to defend myself. A few shovels hang on the wall to my right. I edge over toward them, and the figure follows.

Without much time to consider my choices of weaponry, I snatch a spade-edged shovel and turn on the figure, my weapon raised above my head like a spear. I lunge toward the figure and launch the shovel at it. The makeshift spear makes contact but does not penetrate its body like I'd hoped.

I dart back and grab another shovel. This time, I don't let go of the weapon. Instead, I thrust it forward, feeling the freak's ribs shatter, as the spade impales its chest. The stench coming from it is unbearable, almost as if it meat has been expired for days. The figure staggers back, but I force the shovel in until I see it come out the other side.

22

It pays no attention to its wounds; the thing doesn't seem to care that it has a shovel sticking out from both ends of its body. Its arms continue flailing about, trying to reach me. A war cry leaves my mouth and echoes through the store, as I give the wooden handle a jerk, knocking my attacker off its feet. The monster falls to the ground and lands with thud. The shovel lodges in something on the floor, maybe tile, and pins the body to the ground.

I frantically search the area for a more effective weapon. A sledgehammer stands on the floor like a bamboo tree poking up out of the soil. I pick it up and raise it as high as I can. I bring it down on the thing's head, using its nose as a bulls-eye. The head explodes when the metal makes contact spewing blood, brain matter, and skull fragments everywhere. I vomit again, but yellow stomach acid is all that's left. After I compose myself, I take one last look at the body. The monster's shirt has a name tag covered in blood that reads, *Al*, and below it, *Ask us about our hammers*.

The banging on the door, and the car alarm is driving me crazy. I need to make it back to the shop. I can lock the gates and take the indoor ladder to the roof. I should be able to hole up there, 'til I find out what the hell is going on. The only problem is the outside stairway to the roof. I'll have to destroy it, so the demented can't reach me.

I decide on my plan and begin looking around the store for more items I can convert to weapons. I'll be running a good 50-yards through people, so I'll need something light and sharp. I walk up and down the aisles until I find what I need among the camping supplies: two machetes, still in their packages. I open them and test the sharpness of the blades with my thumb. "They're as sharp as they're going to get."

I wrap my hand around the handle and take a few practice swings. I keep one machete out, and use my belt to tie a sheath to my waist for the second blade. After swinging through the plumbing section, I pick up a pipe wrench and walk to the glass window. The manic group outside is still banging on the door.

Chapter Four

I take a deep breath and launch the wrench through the window. A loud crash rings throughout the store when the glass shatters. Instantly, the muffled car alarm and moans grow louder in the store.

All the demented outside look toward the broken window, then look at me. I spring to life. I exit the store through the shattered window and run for the shop. Hands try to reach me from every direction, as I speed by them.

I swing the machete as I run, severing arms and other limbs like butter. I'm impressed at the fantastic job the machete is doing. I was expecting to have to work harder to sever heads. More of the demented are massed in the pawnshop's driveway. For a brief second, I feel overwhelmed by the smell and shocking numbers that massed here in such a short amount of time. I slice my way through their human wall and make it into the shop. Thankfully, none of them have gotten inside while I've been gone. I close the shatterproof doors and attach the lock. I lower the shutters on the inside of the building and chain them closed, wrapping the chain around one of the machetes to keep it from moving.

Next, I search the safe for any extra rounds. I find six. The pistol is still tightly fastened on my belt next to the second machete. In one swift movement, I grab the Glock and eject the magazine, then load the remaining rounds.

I climb the ladder that leads to the roof and open the hatch door. The car battery must have died because the alarm has shut off. I didn't realize how much the beep muffled the loud moans of the freaks. Using the edge, I pull myself up and close the hatch behind me. I run to the ledge of the building and peer out into the streets. There are thousands of demented on the ground; they swarm toward the pawnshop from every direction.

Now that they know I'm here, they will keep coming after me. I snap out of my daze when I hear moans coming from behind.

"Shit!" I yell, remembering I'd meant to take care of the staircase on the side of the building.

How did they know I was up here? I wonder.

They advance up the stairs by the dozen. The demented in front lose their footing and fall back into the mob but are pushed forward. Others that aren't so lucky are trampled and lost in the advancing crowd. A small portion of the horde find the railing, only to be shoved off the stairs and fall to the hard cement below. I reach for the pistol and fire all six shots but only four of the demented fall. In desperation, I throw the pistol at the group, hitting one of them in the groin.

I glance down, gauging whether I can survive a jump from the roof of the two-story building. Even if I live, I might break a leg; then I'd be dead anyway.

I reach for the handle of the sheathed machete. My only option is to fight them all. I know it's a losing battle, but it's the only chance I have.

I begin with the demented closest to me. My violent swing decapitates two of them, their heads fall off their bodies. Blood squirts out of the gaping wounds like a fountain. A group of five waits directly behind the headless forms. Kicking the still standing form, I wait for them to approach. I'm covered in blood; it causes the handle on my machete to stick. I swing and take off three more scalps before another group of four approaches. I'm starting to trip over the bodies on the ground. I swing at one of the demented, and the machete lodges in its collar bone. Its mouth snaps at my hand. I jerk and pull, trying to free my weapon, but it's no use. The battle is over. One has me from behind; another grasps my ankle. I fall back, and my head lands hard. Two others pile on top of me. I feel teeth sink into my neck and my shin. I screech from the pain. Hands tear at my stomach, ripping it open. The throbbing is unbearable, to the point where I feel only numbness. I stop screaming, as my vision blurs and slowly dims until I see nothing but darkness.

Chapter Five

I wake up from a deep sleep. I'm sitting on a chair, my body leaning on the counter.

"Did I fall asleep?" I ask myself aloud. "Wow, what a crazy dream."

I yawn and look at my watch.

"Almost time to go." I mutter, then laugh. "I can't believe I fell asleep. Good thing I work alone."

I stand, and my cell phone slides off my lap, onto the floor. The battery compartment pops open, and I kneel down to pick up the pieces. A few moments later, every part in its proper place, I stand back up and face the showroom. Maggie, the old woman from my dream, is standing in front of me. The 14-karat gold Figaro Link necklace dangles from her hand.

Was it really a dream or a premonition of what's to come? I was never a believer in the paranormal, but that dream felt real. It felt genuine, as if I were meant to kill. The rush I got when I decapitated those demented was astonishing.

Maggie continues to stare at me with her caring eyes. I can't do anything other than stare back. I'm dumbfounded by the way I pictured Maggie in my mind; my vision was spot on. The only difference is, that in my dream she was wearing a blue sweater. In reality, her sweater is gray, and her hair is done up a bit different.

The elderly woman keeps holding her Figaro Link necklace out toward me, but she still hasn't said a word.

"Hi there, can I help you?" I manage to ask.

"Hello, young man. How much can I get for this necklace?"

I stare at her for another moment. I'm wondering if I should take her again or be honest. When we did this in my dream, it didn't end well for either of us.

"How much are you looking to get?" I ask, going back into pawnbroker mode.

"Well," she says, as a mournful look washes over her face, "My granddaughter, Martha, just died, and I need at least two hundred dollars to help with her funeral costs."

I'm starting to think my dream meant something. My facts are a bit off; it was her son that died in my dream, now it's her granddaughter. I did get the main idea down, someone close to her died. Is this some kind of supernatural event? What other explanation is there? I don't know this lady; we've never met. Still, the skeptic in me is not totally convinced yet.

"I am so sorry to hear that," I say, but this time my sympathy is real. "How are you holding up?"

"I'm fine," she replies.

"Mind if I ask how it happened?" She looks at me with a frown. "Sorry, I… I didn't mean to pry."

"It's okay, Martha passed away yesterday morning, she was eaten to death."

An unseen force slaps me across the chest as my brain processes the words. "Excuse me?" I ask with shock and fright in my voice. "Did you say she was eaten to death?"

"She was beaten to death, by a monster."

I let out a sigh of relief. My mind is searching for any form of connection it can. "I'm so sorry to hear that." Here's my chance to get more information out of her. "What is your name, ma'am?"

"My name is Maggie Bliss," she says with a Scottish accent.

I laugh at the sudden change in tone, then reach for her necklace. I'm mostly trying to hide the fact that I'm terrified. Working in a pawnshop molds you into a heartless person. I can hide all my emotions so no one knows something's bothering me.

I weigh the necklace. The scale reads out at 26.6 grams. I scratch the necklace against a testing stone and pour a drop of testing acid on the scratch. The necklace tests at 14 karats. I'm finally becoming a believer, but why is this happening to me? Was it a vision of my future? If I continue to take people for their gold, will ravenous cannibals consume me?

I turn back to face Maggie. "Have we ever met before?"

"No, I don't think so," she replies. "I can't be sure, though. I suffer from long-term memory loss."

I want to give her the full money to which she's entitled. But I know if I do, my bosses will ream me once they see today's reports. I can't afford to get fired. She's only asking for two hundred dollars. I'll give her that.

I smile at Maggie. "I just did the math, and it looks like I'll be able to give you two hundred dollars for the necklace."

A malicious grin comes over her face. "Are you sure that's all I can get, Marky-B?" she asks, in a raspy demonic voice.

My chest feels empty, as soon as I hear that voice. I'm too frightened to reply.

"Don't you mean that I deserve $320.00?" she asks with that same voice.

Am I dreaming again or is this real?

Dement

Maggie's face begins to shift into the face of the monster she became in my vision. Blood from her body seeps through the gray sweater. A large slash expands on her neck; blood squirts out like a fountain and splashes across my black work shirt. Her eyes turned that memorizing shade of red.

I stagger back when the blood splashes across my body. I can't take my eyes away from this monster. I knew there was something more to my dream, but I didn't want to believe it. The demented were real, and Maggie has turned into one of them. If this is a dream, I hope I wake before I destroy Maggie. Even though she is a vicious flesh-eating monster, there's something about this old lady that draws me.

I snap out of my daze when Maggie gives out a loud screech. I search around for anything I can use. In my dream, destroying the brain brought them down. I hope it's the same here.

An electric chainsaw lies on the floor. I took it in on pawn earlier today. I pick up the tool and plug the 10-foot extension cord into an electrical socket. The chainsaw roars to life. That feeling of excitement returns, as my body fills with epinephrine.

Maggie skirts the counter and staggers toward me. I only have ten feet to work with. I can't move. Her gray skin glows beneath the store's fluorescent lights. The blood all over her body is dry, and the smell coming from her is awful. I try to inhale through my mouth and exhale through my nose.

I swing the chainsaw left to right, trying to catch Maggie in the arc of the blade. She stops just out of reach, glares at me, and then smiles. Blood drips out of her mouth and free-falls to the ground.

"Do you remember now?" Maggie asks, in a deep, gargled voice.

"No. You're just a fucking crazy woman."

Maggie throws her head back and laughs.

"That is correct, Mark. I am inside of you. I am the voice in your head,"

"What do you mean?"

"I mean nothing. This is a dream. Everything here means nothing. You're going crazy, Mark. How much longer can you go without real food or fresh drinking water? It's only a matter of time before you jump off the roof and become lunch for all of us."

I have no idea what Maggie is chattering about. What roof?

"For how long can you hear the moans? You can hear them all, can't you?"

I brandish the chainsaw, but its noise seems to quiet as hundreds of different moans sound in my ear. I shake my head, but the moans continue.

"Stop it!" I yell.

"Don't be so surprised. That's all you've been hearing for the past few months. Can you stand another few or maybe even a year?" She laughs again. "They are never going away, Mark. They know you're here and won't stop until they devour every last bit of you." Maggie throws her head back and laughs uncontrollably.

The moans begin to quiet, until all I can hear is Maggie's demonic laugh. I pull the acceleration trigger on the chainsaw, and it roars, drowning out Maggie's laughter. I yank the cord from the wall and swing the chainsaw at Maggie. She's caught off guard, and the still-circulating chainsaw rips though half her neck, before lodging fast between her vertebrae. I yank back and forth with all my strength and feel the chainsaw loosening.

Maggie's arms swing violently toward me, but I keep my distance as best as possible. I raise my leg and kick her in the chest, and the chainsaw breaks loose. She stumbles backward toward the wall. Her head sways to the right, blood gushing from her hacked neck. The spinal cord is visible, and I can see where the chainsaw lodged.

I run toward Maggie, hoping I don't trip over the cord. I swing my weapon like a club and feel her bones snap.

Maggie's head rolls off her body and hits the floor. I stare at the head as it makes its way toward the counter, smearing a line of dark red blood on the floor. The head stops rolling with Maggie's lifeless face looking back at me. One eye is open; the other twitches. Her jaw falls open, and a black tongue flops out of her mouth.

I drop the chainsaw on the floor. I'm breathing hard, and my eyes are watery. A humming noise rises from Maggie's severed head. Her mouth and eyes move. I reel back in fright and stare at her detached head.

"If you survived this, then you're the one," the head whispers.

Chapter Six

I awake from my torturous sleep in the black tent that I set up on the roof of the pawnshop. My heart is racing, and my body is sore. The staircase is destroyed, and down below are thousands of hungry dements. Not one second goes by that I don't hear a moan.

I stagger out of the one-person tent and squint as the morning sunlight hits my face. Fumbling in my jeans pockets for my sunglasses, I find them in three pieces.

"Great," I mutter.

I force my eyes open, so they can adjust to the light, instantly feeling a headache coming on. I peer over the ledge at the half-rotted walking corpses. They are still clawing at the building walls trying to reach me. I turn away and snatch my backpack off the back of a lawn chair. I sit on the chair and search the bag for canned food. My cell phone rests inside a side pocket. It's been useless since the first day of the outbreak. I think about tossing the device, but I can't shake the voice that tells me to hold on to it. A can of sardines and a Fiber One bar are all that remain in the bag. I work the can opener, then eat the sardines with my fingers, taking my time, trying to fill up on what I have. I finish the sardines and then wolf down the Fiber One bar. I toss the metal can over the ledge.

I've been stuck up here since that dreadful day I met, Maggie Bliss. She was attacked after I took her necklace. Unlike in my dream, I didn't help her. I cowered and climbed up to the roof, taking everything I could with me. I destroyed the staircase that led up to the roof, then set up my little camp. Luckily someone had recently pawned a lot of camping equipment.

I dream about that day often. Sometimes, I have dreams within dreams. Last night, I had the dream where I actually went to help Maggie. I found my way into Al's Hardware, fought with Al and laughed at his name tag. Then, I ran back over here and got eaten by the things.

The machetes are always my favorite part in the dream. Even if I had some now, I don't think I'd be brave enough to use them. In my dreams I'm fearless, but in reality, I'm lucky I didn't shit myself when I first saw them.

I don't have any more food. I'm going to have to go

on a supply run, but every time I do, it draws more of them to my building. Even though I only go to the building next door, the demented seem to double. I don't know where they're coming from.

I crawl into the tent and check my FM radio to see if anything is broadcast. Nothing has been heard for the past few weeks, but I still check every day in case something comes up.

The first radio broadcasts were frantic. No one knew why the dead were rising. The last I heard, they still didn't know. Half of Bluebird County's population was infected in the first 24 hours. I was too busy haggling with Maggie to notice the chaos outside. This infection, whatever it is, moves fast. When Maggie was attacked, she rose to her feet in a matter of minutes. At first, I saw her demented body clawing at the building trying to reach me. When more of them showed up, she vanished into the crowd.

I don't know why she's always in my dreams, telling me that I can't kill all of them. Maybe I just feel guilty for hustling her. I was only doing my job. I just hope the dreams and their moans stop; I want everything to stop. Mental note: next time I go get supplies, look for headphones.

I flip through the radio channels. I'm surprised to find something playing. It's the Manny Mayhem Morning Show. I can't believe they are back on the air.

When this whole mess started, the radio show cast locked themselves in the building. Manny is one crazy motherfucker. They all are. I got most of my information from them, and someone who called in named, Joe. I owe a lot to that caller, he went over the basic stuff like killing them, and how slow they are. He said he was a cameraman for the news and that's how he found out about the dead. No one could ever agree on what to call them. The word zombie, did cross my mind, they do have many similarities. They eat flesh, follow noises and destroying the brain brings them down. But zombie is a term that belongs in a movie. Manny likes to call them freaks; I call them demented. No one knows what they really are, so one name is as good as any. I turn up the volume to get a better listen.

"All right, everyone who hasn't been eaten yet. I'm glad you're still listening. We haven't had a caller in a long time, mostly because we took some time off the airways. I got some good news and bad news to report. The good news is that I finally fucked our news girl, Cowgirl Kelly, and man what a lay. The bad news is that our producer, Petite Pete, blew his brains out, after he started showing signs of the infection. His body is in a bathroom stall. We don't use that shitter anymore. The stunt boy known as, Babylon, painted 'RIP' on the door.

Speaking of Babylon, that boy has seen his last day.

A freak got him while he was trying to round one up for our, 'What's a Zombie Thinking?' bit. I'm not sure where everyone else ran off to. The only ones here are myself, Manny Mayhem, and the lovely Reverse Cowgirl Kelly. Why don't you say hello to the listeners?"

No noise comes out of the radio speaker for a lengthy moment. Finally, I hear a female moan come out of the brown box. Even though I've been hearing their moans for the past few months, hearing one come out of the radio was chilling. Manny has totally lost it.

"Now, now," Manny continues. "Before everyone starts asking questions, we had sex after she turned. Boy was she a biter. She got me on the neck. Man she was rough. She even nibbled a piece of my prick off. Ha, Ha, Just playin'. But remember how I always tried to get her to sleep with me? She always said, 'over my dead body'. Well ..."

I turn off the radio in disgust. I don't feel like listening to the ramblings of a crazy infected person. I crawl out of the tent and put my filthy work shirt on. I swing the empty backpack onto my back.

Next to the pawnshop is a little 99 cent store. I've almost cleaned the place out; so, I'll need to find somewhere else to get food supplies, soon. Only other place I know of is the Vons at the end of Scandon Avenue. There's no way I'll make it all the way over there with this crowd.

I stretch my legs and prepare to jump to the next building. The buildings are only separated by a three-foot gap. I run and jump off the ledge. My feet hit the gravel. I slip and come crashing down, hitting my head on the roof. I'm always falling when I land. This time, I didn't break any skin. I get up and dust myself off. My head doesn't hurt, but I should try to find some Ibuprofen, just in case.

Most of the buildings on this road have easy access to the roof by a ladder. I walk to the roof hatch and open it. This place was empty from the start, so I don't have to worry about the demented. I always quietly grab what I need and get out. That seems to have worked fine, so far.

I make my way down the ladder step-by-step. The only light in the building comes from the large front window. I can see silhouettes of the demented moving about outside. I make my way to the grocery section and fill the backpack with whatever is left. I search the medicine aisle and grab anything that is intended to ease headaches. I turn back to look for headphones. I find some at the front of the store next to the tinted window.

The demented shamble across the sidewalk in front of the store. One of them brushes up against the glass. A smear of goo marks its trail, as it walks from one end of the window to the other. I stagger back and bump into a stand of music CD's. The stand falls to the ground with a loud crash. Each CD makes its own clatter, as it hits the floor. I am overwhelmed with anger at myself, as I hear the first hand slam on the glass window.

I suspect that the glare bouncing off the window shields me from being noticed. The demented don't need to see in order to follow something. That's why they haven't left this area; I make too much damn noise on the roof. Not to mention the fact that I stand on the ledge and yell at them, sometimes. It's a good way to relieve stress and anger.

Another arm hits the window, followed by another. Before long, hundreds of hands pound on the glass window. I look around the room, scanning the area for anything else I need to grab in case the glass breaks. If the window shatters, and they get in, there's no way I'll be able to return to this store.

My backpack is almost full. I throw in a few bottles of warm water and zip up the bag; it's better than no water. I hear the glass beginning to crack, and a moment later it shatters. I put the backpack on and look toward the window just in time to see shards of glass impale the bodies of the first wave. Hundreds of them push forward, trampling over the unlucky few in front. They form an undead wall, unwittingly enabling the dements in the back to climb into the store. The moans grow louder; they see me, and they know I'm food.

In seconds, dozens of them make their way into the store, mouths open and arms outstretched. I turn and bolt for the ladder. The speed of the demented accelerates. I notice them closing in on me. As much as I want to fight them, I know I'm outnumbered, and I have nothing to fight with. I make my way up the wooden ladder on the far wall. Their arms swipe for me, but I'm just out of reach.

Sweat falls down my face, as I continue to climb the two-story-long ladder. I'm almost to the top when I feel the ladder shake. I look down to see an endless barrage of demented clawing at the ladder. I continue to press on, but so do the demented. They see me on the ladder, and somehow, they know that if that ladder falls, I'll come down with it.

I lose my footing, as one of the steps breaks under my feet. I grip on with my hands, as my legs frantically search for another step. My feet can't find one; both legs dangle now. I try to lift myself with my arms, but I'm too weak to do it. I feel the ladder crumble beneath me. Hundreds more of the demented pour into the room; all of them want me. I hold on as best I can, but my palms are sweaty. I'm starting to slip. With all my strength, I try to pull myself up but, my grip loosens, and I'm pushed down by an unseen power. My legs lodge between two rungs. My whole body falls back, and I'm left hanging upside-down on the ladder.

I look at all of the demented staring, trying to reach any part of me. Blood rushes to my head, and I can feel it taking effect. The freaks quiet down and clear a path. In the sudden silence, I hear footsteps, and I can make out the shadow of a person approaching. Soon enough I see the body of a frail old woman.

It's Maggie. Is she controlling the dead?

"Well …," Maggie starts, in her raspy demonic voice, "how many of us can you kill from up there?"

Damn, why does she have to talk? I have never heard any of them talk, except for Maggie, and then only in my dreams. Could I be dreaming again? I slip the backpack off, and it falls to the floor, hitting a demented on top of its head.

"I can't do anything from up here. I'm trapped," I answer, out of breath.

"You're trapped just like on the roof. You can't stay there, forever. What do you plan to do?"

"I can't do anything, unless I kill all of you. I know I'm dreaming, and when I wake up, I'm getting out of here. I'm getting off the roof. I'm going to kill you or die trying."

I jerk my body in an attempt to dislodge my trapped foot. I feel it loosen, so I continue to wiggle.

"I'm glad to hear that, Mark. I'll mold you into the person you are meant to be. Now, get down and kill us all, if you can."

The demented wait hungry below. Maggie is no longer visible, it's as if she dissipated into the air. My foot slips out of my shoe, and I fall to the floor. I lie flat on my back, and the demented close in to huddle around me.

Chapter Seven

My eyes open, and I see the clear blue sky. The moans of the demented continue to ring in my ears, as I sit up. I'm on the roof of the 99 cent store, where I slipped and hit my head.

"Fucking dreams need to stop," I mutter, as I rub the back of my head.

A large black bird descends to the roof. It lands on the ledge that looks out over the demented-filled street. It crows and looks in my direction. I'm instantly reminded of Edgar Allen Poe's poem, *The Raven*.

"Is there Balm in Gilead?" I recite to the bird, and then laugh quietly.

It looks away and crows twice.

"Do you know of any distant aidenns around here?"

The bird looks at me and crows again. It extends its wings, flapping them incessantly as though the creature is communicating with me.

"I wish I had your wings, buddy," I say. "Do you know if anyone else is alive?"

The bird crows a final time and takes flight, heading west. I watch the animal until its black form blends with the sky. I hear a faint noise over the moans of the dead. I look behind me and see dozens of helicopters in the sky. All of them are headed west; the same direction as the bird.

I stand up and flap my arms, screaming at the helicopters. I'm too far down to be heard, but now I know there are other survivors nearby. The Pacific Ocean is only ten or so miles west from here. There's no way those helicopters have enough fuel to take them across it. Other survivors have to be between here and there. I need to get off the roof and head west, but first I need to gather my supplies. I'll plan my escape tonight.

I walk toward the hatch and open it. The smell of rotting flesh and decay hits me like a wave of filth. I peer down the ladder and notice moving figures.

The demented have made their way into the 99 cent store. My only source of provisions. Looks like I'll need to make my plans on an empty stomach. As I peer down the hatch, I make out a much-too-familiar figure. My heart drops, as I stare at Maggie, who is now staring back at me. Loose skin from her neck hangs down to her side. Her eyes glow a faint red. A loud scream erupts from her mouth, as more demented enter the room. They lunge for the ladder, shaking it violently. One of them makes a clumsy attempt to climb it.

The hideous monster climbing the ladder is all I need to see. I shut the hatch door and look for something to help keep it closed. Before I can locate a weight, the hatch door swings opens, revealing a hideous demented head.

Its skin is pale gray, and a deep scar engraves its cheek. Its eyes glow red as it opens its mouth to expose brown, rotting teeth. An unnerving moan surges out of the creature's mouth, and the thing slowly lifts itself onto the roof. As its second foot hits the roof, I hear the sound of the ladder breaking, and a moan followed by a faint splat.

This is the first time I've ever seen one of them do something like this and I don't like it. The monster, on the roof with me, lifts his arms and growls. Mucous bubbles out of its nose and like an infant, it doesn't do anything to clear it. I glance around for something, anything I can use to take this monster down. There's nothing here but gravel.

As my gaze swings toward the pawnshop building, it lights on the television antenna at the corner of the roof. I run toward it, as the demented shuffles in my direction. I yank at the antenna, until it comes free.

I know this is not a dream, yet I'm suddenly filed

with courage. Normally, I wouldn't get near one of the demented. I would just jump to the pawnshop roof and hope it would fall off the ledge. I stop questioning my actions and race toward the monster.

I gag when I notice its intestines poking out of tear in its stomach, but I press on, using the V-shaped end of the antenna to keep the dement at a distance. I shuffle the creature over to the ledge, where I hope to push it over. At that moment, something inside of its stomach erupts, spewing blood and body fat onto the rooftop next to me. I gag again and stagger back. The dement uses this as an opportunity to push himself toward me. I feel the end of the antenna giving way and I know I need to push the dement over the edge, before it breaks. It's only a step away from being pushed over, when something larger erupts in its stomach.

Yellow pus and blood spew onto my arms and shirt. A clump of entrails lodges on the antenna. I feel the nausea kick in, but before I can vomit, I need to push the thing over. I gather all my strength to give one last heave. I manage to push the dement off the edge. It grabs the antenna and takes it with him, as it descends to the pit of living dead.

The dement hits the ground, knocking down one of its brothers, while the antenna pole hits another. I see its head hit the pavement and explode, leaving behind a pool of unclean blood. I vomit the sardines off the roof.

My vomit spews onto the demented below, like chunky yellow rain.

Once I compile myself, I make my way back toward the roof hatch. I open it, expecting to see Maggie's horrid face, but she is nowhere to be seen. Dozens of the demented litter the small room. The ladder is broken, so I don't have to worry about them getting up here.

I look down at my blood and pus-stained shirt. Blood and little bits of tendon continue to drizzle down my arms, I wipe it on my shirt and pants. I hadn't noticed before, but the blood smells sweet, almost like candy. I take in a big gust of wind. I start to feel disoriented; my head pounds, and my temperature spikes. The dizziness brings me to my knees, and I roll face-up on the roof.

"Is this it?" I ask myself. "Am I infected?"

I'm facing west, and I see dark rain clouds move in. I think about how thirsty I am, and then laugh, just before my eyelids close. I finally feel a momentary peace, as I drift back into my dreams.

Chapter Eight

I don't know how long I've been lying here, but I know something is terribly wrong. I feel numb, and my stomach grumbles for nourishment. The sky looks different, as well. Everything shines with a red tint. Large gusts of wind rage around me, blowing my hair in disarray. I am cold, and I see gray clouds cover the once blue sky.

I slowly sit up and look at my surroundings. I'm on top of a roof, but it doesn't look like the pawnshop roof. I know I'm on Scandon, but I'm a little further down. The bursts of wind calm, as I hear the storm carry voices. Human voices cry out in pain, in the distance. I hear them and every impulse in my body drives me to find that noise. I stagger up to my feet, I look down and see dry blood smeared on my shirt. I'm having difficulty moving, my body is sore and tender. I attempt to walk toward the ledge of the roof, but my body wants to

go a different direction. After walking for a few moments, I make it to the edge of the roof and peer out to
the demented below. None of them pay any attention to
me. It's as if I'm no longer up here.

I try to talk, but no sound comes out. My throat instantly feels sore as I attempt to use my vocal cords,
again. A low and soft moan leaves my mouth. I begin to
panic inside my mind. Could it be true? Have I turned
into one of the monsters?

A violent gust of wind blows, the force nearly
pushes me off the roof. I hear another human cry, as the
wind pushes by. I stare in the direction of the scream,
and my stomach grumbles. I feel my mouth water at the
sound of food.

It starts raining, heavy and thick raindrops smash
against the top of my head. I begin walking toward the
noise. It's coming from the west, and my feet move in
that direction. After a few steps, I notice that I am almost to the edge of the roof, and I don't feel a desire to
stop. I just want to continue walking in that direction.

I reach the end of the roof and take a step off. My
body rushes down toward the street. My eyes close, as I
hit the ground with a thud. I land on my back, but I
don't feel any pain. Instead, I feel the need to sit up and
continue walking in the direction of the cries.

I stumble to my feet and look down. A pool of
blood sits where I landed. I look forward and then, to

my left. A store window casts my reflection, and I can finally see myself.

The reflection staring back at me, is not me. Not in the sense of being a demented, but the person in the mirror is not me. I have black hair, and my reflection says I'm a blond. My nose is also incorrect, and my face does not have high cheek bones, like this person. My jaw is broken, and the bottom half of my mouth hangs to one side. Blood gushes out of my mouth and nose, then drips down my chin. I quickly look away.

I have not noticed but the rain has completely stopped, and I am alone. The clouds are also gone, and it's a sunny day. All of the other demented have shambled their way up Scandon Avenue and out of view. All of them are chasing that beautiful cry. I follow, far behind them, in that direction.

I come up to a familiar building. It's the 99 cent store. I ignore the window, which I know is casting my reflection, and continue walking. Something to my left catches my eye. It's a woman. She's walking out of a building and doesn't notice me. She slowly walks to the street and turns west. She doesn't move fast, even I can catch her. I follow the woman.

She is almost within reach, but still doesn't notice me. I'm there, I reach for her and force her to the ground. The woman looks up at me and in horror, I see that it's Maggie. She cries out for help, but I open my mouth and sink my teeth into the side of her neck. I chew and swallow the delicious meat. I lean in to take another bite. Blood gushes out of every wound in Maggie's body. I pay no attention to the blood spraying on me and continue eating.

A male voice screams at the top of his lungs.

Someone else for me to eat. This though pleases me.

Maggie has already died from the blood loss. She lies motionless on the ground, as I look up at the man. The sun shining down behind him makes me unable to distinguish who it is. Even though I know the man standing there is me, I still want to see his face.

I slowly rise to my feet. I am able to see the man, but it doesn't look like me. I look toward the glass entrance of the pawnshop and it is closed.

This isn't me, It's not even a man, it's a woman.

I stare at her face, as someone sneaks up behind me and puts something over my head. I see nothing but darkness, as I am kicked off my feet and dragged, somewhere.

I hear the engine of a car start and doors slam shut. Three voices start talking amongst themselves. I'm trying hard to understand what they are saying, but my ears aren't working properly.

After a short ride, the engine shuts off. The doors open, and I am dragged out by my feet. The three continue to talk, as I am dragged out onto concrete. I hear a door creak open. My head bounces over a ledge, and the hard floor turns into a carpet. I'm propped up and forced to sit on a chair. I can feel the muscles in my legs rip, my body is no longer meant to be limber.

I'm tied to a chair, and the black sack is removed from my head. I instantly begin snapping my teeth toward my captors. There are two females and one male. One of the females and the male are dressed in the same black battle dress uniform. The other woman is dressed in jeans and a hooded sweatshirt. They begin talking amongst themselves, but this time I can hear them clearly.

"What do you wanna do with it first?" one of the females asks the male.

"I don't know, Holloway," he replies.

The other female enters the conversation. "Well, we caught it cause you wanted it, Walker. You said you wanted to study it, so get to work. There are thousands of them outside, so we better come up with something soon."

"In time, Williams," Walker replies, then continues, "Let's try seeing if it understands us."

Walker looks into my eyes and asks, "What is your name?"

I look back at the man and let out a moan. I try to answer, but I can't form the correct words.

The female, named Holloway, walks closer to me.

She leans in, as I snap at her, I try to descend my teeth into her neck. She laughs at my attempt. I am being held down by bonds. She continues to laugh and leaves her head inches away from my reach. At that moment, I yank at my bonds, and my wrist breaks loose, giving me the extra inch I need.

I sink my teeth into the woman's neck, prying skin free. She yells and staggers back. Panic ensues in the room, and Walker kicks me in the chest, knocking the chair backwards. I lie there chewing my prize meat, as I see Williams walk toward me with a pistol in her hand. She raises the weapon at me and empties her magazine in my abdomen. I feel the force of the bullets, but don't feel any pain.

"You have to get them in the head," Walker says, as he walks toward me with his pistol.

I look toward him, as he raises his weapon. I moan at him, then he squeezes the trigger.

Chapter Nine

Rain hits my face causing my eyes to flutter open. The water must have washed away all of the infected blood. The sweet aroma is gone, it is masked by the smell of wet pavement. That candy smell, from the blood, must have made me pass out. Maybe their blood works as an anesthesia. I slowly stand to my feet, as I begin to think about the dream I just had. They always feel real, but when I wake up, I know the reality of everything.

"It's all just dreams." I tell myself. But I know I'm slowly losing my mind.

Being stuck up here for months, listening to the constant moans would make anyone go mad. I'm surprised I haven't taken Maggie's advice and jumped off the roof. I still have some will to live, I need to get off this roof and maybe, I can head west and find other survivors.

I walk to the edge of the roof and look down at the demented. The one I pushed off the roof still lies on its back. The antenna rests a few feet away from it. The surrounding demented bump into the metal pole pushing it around.

I take a few steps back and look toward the pawnshop roof. I sprint toward the ledge and heave myself to the other building. I land perfectly and continue to walk toward my tent. I crawl inside and zip the entrance. I'm soaking wet, but I crawl under my blankets, anyway. I'm hungry, and I have no food. I'm cold and wet, but I have no dry clothes. If I wasn't so scared, I'd go back into the pawnshop.

Maybe it's fully secure, and they can't get in, the thought repeats in my head.

I realize something, as I lie under the wet blankets. I'm not scared anymore. After I fought the demented on the roof, I have no reason to be afraid. I held my ground against one. Then, I thought about the thousand down below. I leave the thought of going back into the pawnshop. There's stuff in there I'll need. I can't risk having them find a way into the store if they hear me inside. I sit up and begin to plan my escape.

If I'm properly prepared, I should be able to outrun them, if I can get them to spread out. I start thinking about what I have in the store. I know there are power tools, gas tools, lawnmowers, and chainsaws. There are a lot of useless items: jewelry, DVDs, and video game systems. The thought of heading back down to the shop enters my head again. I have no choice; it's been so long since I've been down there, I forgot everything the shop has to offer.

I throw the blankets off of me and unzip the tent. Being enclosed in the tent, muffled their moans. I can hear them, again. Hopefully, the rain and wind will help mask my noise. I exit the tent and walk toward the hatch. I unlock it and open the little door. The ladder stares back at me, but the room is dark. I doubt the power is still on, so I might have to do everything in the dark.

I take my first step onto the ladder and slowly, make my way down. I stop every few steps and listen. I don't hear anything, the room is quiet. I make it down and slowly, walk to the front counter, looking behind me, constantly.

There are flashlights under the counter. I find a Maglite and flick it on. The room illuminates with light, and I do a quick search of the building.

Nothing has made its way inside. I can't hear the others outside either. All I hear is the rain. I walk to the back storage room where we keep all the pawns. The shelves line up parallel to each other. Each spot on the shelf is covered with usable items.

One row carries circular saws. I can use the blades

and throw them at the demented. I take the saws to the front of the shop. I walk back to the storage room and continue to look for useful items.

After walking back and forth for hours, I have a vast assortment of items. I begin taking the objects and making them useful. I drain the gasoline out of the lawnmowers and pour the liquid into glass jars. I take apart circular saws and place the blades on the counter. Then, I take the useless parts back to the storage room.

There are some nail guns but without an air compressor they are useless. Without power, an air compressor is useless. My useable items pile is quickly dulling out. After figuring out what I can and can't use, I end up with: four Molotov cocktails, one chainsaw with a full tank, a two gallon jug of reserve fuel, circular saw blades, two store bought Katanas, a sledge hammer, and many large objects to launch off the roof.

Getting all the TVs and air compressors to the roof is a challenge. I manage to tie a rope around them and pull them up to the roof through the ladder door. Some items are too big, so I'm only able to get the smaller stuff onto the roof.

Five hours later, I am fully armed and ready to make a path through the undead. All of my weapons are on the roof waiting for the right time.

There is one item I'm missing. The Glock 17 that is in the store's safe. I completely forgot about it. My dreams have really messed up my views on reality. I walk to the safe, punch in the code, and yank the handle. The door swings open and on the left, I see the holster. I grab the firearm and the ammunition. I have one fully loaded magazine, and an empty one sits next to the holster. I load the remaining rounds into the empty magazine and put it in my pocket. There are just enough cartridges to load the second magazine. I leave the safe open and walk back to the ladder. I climb up and close the hatch behind me. I am exhausted and so very hungry. I try to forget everything because tomorrow, rain or shine, I will be getting off this roof.

It stopped raining a while ago, so hopefully by tomorrow morning everything will be clear. I take the Glock to the tent and set it next to a pillow. I turn and walk toward the edge. Peering out onto the street, I see the thousands of hungry monsters. They notice me and claw at the building. One of them catches my gaze; Maggie is in the crowd staring at me. I shiver and walk back to the tent.

It's getting dark, I'm not sure what time of day it is, but I feel tired and sleepy. I crawl back into the tent and forget everything. Tomorrow will be the day I stand up to all of them and show how insane I've become. My heavy eyelids close, as I drift into a peaceful sleep.

* * *

The sound of birds chirping wakes me from my slumber. The sun is out, and I can see the rays shining down through a few holes in the tent. I sit up, and the first thought in my head is if I'm dreaming. I look around and notice the Glock next to the pillow. I listen carefully as the noise of the birds fade, and the moans of the dead rise. I'm not dreaming. I pick up the Glock and crawl out.

I turn to look at all my weapons, everything is there and ready for my orders. I stand and stretch my legs. I walk toward the ledge, again and look down. I follow what I can see of the road west, toward the direction of the helicopters.

I think about what I have to use as weapons. I know this building is made out of solid concrete bricks. No wood, so the building will survive with a fire blazing next to it. I walk back to my weapons stash and grab two Molotovs. I need to make a clearing, before I head down with a rope harness.

I light the cloth on one of the Molotovs and chuck it below. The bottle breaks, and a cloud of fire spreads amongst them. The demented in the immediate area of ground zero catch on fire. The fire doesn't seem to bother them. They continue to walk bumping into their nearby buddies. Each one that comes in contact with a flaming monster catches on fire. I stand back and light the other cloth. I toss it as far east as possible. The glass bottle breaks, as another fire breaks out. I look down toward the demented in front of the building. The fire is quickly dying out. The wet clothes of the demented must be preventing further flames. I grab another Molotov and launch it back to the dying fire. The bottle breaks spewing gas on the street. The fire continues to roar, as the liquid catches.

I run back to get the last Molotov but stop. I look at the can of reserve fuel I have. I need to lighten my load if I'm going to outrun these things. I grab the can and heave it as far east as possible, hitting one of the demented on fire. The plastic jug falls to the ground. I wait for a second staring at the jug. It catches fire, and a moment later it explodes. The force knocks some off their feet, but most are completely incinerated.

I look back down, and the fire is still raging. The ground is littered with fallen demented on fire. They lie motionless, as the inferno consumes their rotting existence. I light the last Molotov and launch it toward a group of untouched demented. I walk away from the ledge to retrieve the sledge hammer. I hold it over the edge and let it drop. The hammer comes crashing down and hits a still walking dement on the top of the head. The dement falls to the ground, and the hammer lies next to it, out of the fire's reach.

The only thing left to do is sit back and let the fire die out. Once it's out, I can throw the big items I have at the remaining few. I take one last look at the fire below. Maggie is standing just out of the fire's reach. She looks at the blaze, then stares at me. I find my pistol and point it at her. This time she's not going anywhere. I squeeze the trigger, a bullet travels toward Maggie and hits her clear in the forehead. Her body falls forward and instantly catches the blaze. The one who has tormented me is now gone. If the bullet didn't kill her, the fire will.

I walk back to the lawn chair and sit. I have some time before the fire dies, and I'm celebrating Maggie's death with a rest. The Glock stays firmly in my grip, as I lean back and close my eyes.

The first sight in my head is the horrid face of Maggie. A sudden rage fills me, something I've never felt before. She's never going to let me go. I raise the gun to my head and pull the trigger.

Chapter Ten

The sound of an approaching helicopter wakes me. I don't know what's real anymore. Am I truly awake now? Will I ever stop dreaming about Maggie and the demented? I unzip the tent and crawl outside. A low flying helicopter hovers over the demented on the street. I look over to my supplies and everything is still there.

I howl and wave my arms around trying to get their attention. The pilot looks directly at me. A man holding a very large machine gun, points at me through the side opening.

"Are you infected?" I hear over the intercom.

I shake my head: no and yell, "Hungry!"

The helicopter moves toward an open area and hovers over it. The demented, for the first time in months, look away from me and shamble toward the landing helicopter. The man fires his automatic weapon on the advancing crowd. Blood and bits of flesh spew everywhere, as the bullets rip their bodies to shreds. The noise from the weapon is loud, but I don't think they care if they attract attention. None of the demented are able to reach the helicopter. The man stops firing.

"Can you make it to us?" the man asks over the intercom.

I search around the roof for the Glock. I find it and hustle toward the chainsaw. I wrap it around my shoulder with the leather strap. Grabbing the sledge hammer, I toss it over the edge of the roof and see the demented thinning out, as they walk toward the helicopter. I tie the rope to a metal pole sticking out of the roof and put the harness on. I walk to the edge, again and without hesitation jump off.

I hold onto the harness, as I slowly repel down. I reach the ground, and I'm instantly the monsters' first priority. They begin shambling toward me as I see the twenty pound sledge hammer lying on the ground. I pick it up and begin swinging it, like a bat catching nothing but air. I start walking toward the direction of the helicopter. I hit the closest infected, shattering its bones and knocking them back. I continue swinging with every last bit of strength I have.

Blood spews from their mouths and splatters everywhere around me, as I continue to hit the demented. I feel the handle of the hammer crack. I swing once more, hitting a dement on the side of the head. The handle breaks sending the hammer head through a glass window. I throw the handle to the ground and reach for the chainsaw. At that moment, I remember I never tested this chainsaw when the owner brought it in to pawn. I close my eyes and hope that it starts.

I pull the chain, and the machine roars to life. I begin swinging my weapon at anything that comes close to me. The blade slices through the limbs of the demented, sending more blood and tendons everywhere. I continue to run toward the helicopter not wanting to look back.

Once again, the noise of the heavy machine gun echoes in my ear. I hope a stray bullet doesn't hit me. They must have seen me coming through the crowd, because the shooting stops.

I'm able to see the blades of the helicopter, but the demented continue to claw at me. The chainsaw spits and sputters. The machine stops working through a mid-way decapitation. I kick the dement in the chest, and it falls backward, taking the chainsaw with it. I retrieve my pistol and shoot an approaching dement in the head.

I duck my head and run past the last few demented. I'm finally in a clearing, as I approach the aircraft. The man, holding the machine gun, looks in my direction and yells something. Out of instinct, I look over my shoulder and there stands Maggie. There is something different about her. She looks almost transparent, like a ghost. I brush it off as a trick of the mind.

This was the first time in months Maggie and I are this close to each other. Her eyes glow red at the sight of me. Skin still flaps on the side of her neck. Her jaw snaps, as she begins walking toward me. The demented behind her follow, almost as if in command. I raise my pistol and point it at her head. I pull the trigger. The round enters her head, and a horrified look washes over her face. The bullet explodes out of the back of her head and sprays the dead behind her with brain matter and bits of skull fragments. The elderly woman falls to the ground almost instantly.

I turn and run toward the waiting helicopter. I jump in and take the first available seat I see. The helicopter lifts off the ground hastily. A few moments pass and we are in the air heading in the same direction, as the helicopters I saw yesterday.

The man standing before me looks familiar, but I just can't tell from where. He has short spiked hair and doesn't look to be any older than thirty.

"What's your name?" the man asks.

"Mark Bliss," I answer.

"Do you know what you just did Mark?"

I don't understand the question. I look back at him

with a questionable look.

"You just ran through a horde of walking corpses and survived. We were clearing a path to come closer to you. We told you to wait."

"I heard you say over the intercom to make it to the helicopter. So, I gathered stuff and took off running."

He stares at me for a moment. "No, I said for you to stay put, we were clearing a path. But it doesn't matter now, I guess. You're here, you're safe, but fuck man; I've never seen anyone do that and kill so many at once."

"Why didn't you just land on the roof?" I ask.

"There wasn't enough room for the pilot to land safely. How long have you been up there?"

"I don't know, to tell you the truth. A few months maybe?"

"Well you're lucky. You're the first one we've seen alive in a long time. Have you seen anyone?"

I shake my head. "No, I've been up there alone this entire time. I'm thankful you guys were there."

It suddenly hit me like a gun shot. He's Walker, the man in my dream. There were three of them. If I remember correctly, I bit one, Holloway. The person flying must be Williams. What the hell is going on? Why am I having these visions?

I don't say anything about this to them. I think we will all be better off not knowing that I had a dream with them in it. It won't be a good thing if they think I'm crazy. We spend the next few minutes in silence. I put my head back and finally rest.

* * *

We pass a huge steel wall with guards posted everywhere. There are some demented trying to breach the walls, but the guards bring them down, before they can get in. We land inside this compound. Tents are set up everywhere, and a mass of people run toward the helicopter. The engine stops, as Walker steps out. I stand to my feet and make my way off the helicopter. I'm greeted by friendly people that offer me water and food. I feel like I have just landed in Hawaii.

A man approaches and tells me to follow him. With a bottle of water in one hand, and a freshly cooked hamburger in the other, I'll follow this guy, anywhere. He leads me to a large white tent and stands at the entrance then ushers me in. I step inside, chewing on my hamburger and taking huge drinks from my water. The man quickly leaves.

I look around the tent, and I see a silhouette of a person standing at the tent's entrance. The person approaches, and I quickly realize who it is. It's Maggie.

"No!" I yell, spitting out the freshly chewed hamburger.

I've never felt this level of fear in my life. I stare at her in disbelief. She does the same to me. She doesn't know the horror and torment she put me through.

I drop the bottle of water and fumble around for the Glock in my pocket. I pull it out and raise it toward her head.

A sinister grin comes over her face. Her eyes begin to glow red, and I pull the trigger. The sound echoes in the tent, as her body falls down to ground.

I walk to her body and shoot every last round I have left in the firearm. Her head is nearly gone. I glance out of the entrance. No one is there. Everyone is gone. Am I dreaming again?

Chapter Eleven

The sound from the propellers roaring makes my eyes open, I'm still in the helicopter. I don't think I'm ever going to stop dreaming about this.

"Where are we going?" I ask disoriented.

I look out the window and standing on top of a roof is that fucking bitch, Maggie. I'm instantly filled with rage and anger. It feels like I'll never be free from her. I curse the day, Maggie Bliss, stepped foot into the pawnshop. I try to take another look outside, but Walker steps in front of me.

"Do you see something down there?" He asks, and turns to look.

"Yeah, it's the phantom that won't leave me alone."

He shoots me a questionable look. "Phantom?"

"It all started a few months ago, while I was working at the pawnshop. This lady walks in -" I pause for a moment, not saying a word.

I finally realize that Maggie never went inside the pawnshop. I don't remember her ever stopping by. I lean back and try to remember what really happened. I slap my hand on the side of my head, until something clicks. I remember opening up that day, a few hours later people started running. I thought it was another terrorist attack, so I locked the shutter doors and turned one of the televisions on. The news said the dead were walking, and attacking the living. I had to seek higher ground and wait for rescue. I never saw Maggie until I started dreaming. Maybe she is a ghost, but why is she haunting me? Did I really kill her before I got to the helicopter?

Walker looks at me, puzzled. He's probably wondering why I not talking. The big man opens his mouth to say something, when a loud beeping noise sounds inside the helicopter.

"Hold on, something just hit us, we're going down!" Williams, the female pilot yells.

The helicopter falls at an incredible speed. I shut my eyes, as the man standing by the helicopter opening fumbles for his seat. I open my eyes, and the man is gone, sucked out of the helicopter by its rotation and wind. The helicopter continues to fall. It hits the ground, nose first, crushing the pilot on impact. The belt on the seat, and a mysterious blue glow holds me in place.

As everything stops moving, I unbuckle myself and shimmy out of the wreckage. I don't dare to see the condition Williams is in. I know she's a mess. Walker is nowhere in sight. Poor guy. I can't believe I survived the crash. I check my body for any damage and I'm fine. It's like I wasn't even involved in the wreckage. I slowly begin to walk away from the ruins and head toward a large, blue, two-story house. Something, I can't see is pulling me in that direction. I knock on the door and no one answers. I knock again, nothing.

I turn the knob and cautiously walk inside. The first thing I see is a couch. I walk toward it and set my Glock on a coffee table next to a cooking magazine, then lie down. My body finally begins to ache. I close my eyes for a second, when a noise from upstairs interrupts my rest. I reach for the Glock.

Footsteps slowly come creeping down the stairs. I point my Glock in the direction. The figure notices me.

"Don't shoot," the person says.

It's a woman, probably in her late twenties. She raises her arms up in the air and slowly walks toward me.

"You're alive," She says, "I saw your helicopter go down. I'm glad someone survived that. It's been a long time since I've seen anyone normal."

I don't say a word, but I put the pistol down.

"Are you hungry?" She asks, "I have food, I was about to make dinner, wanna join me?"

I nod, as she wonders down to what I assume is the kitchen. I follow her. The strong smell of cinnamon is forceful in the air. I stagger back away from the scent.

The young woman notices my dislike. "Are you some kind of Vampire? One that instead of garlic, doesn't like cinnamon?" she laughs.

"Sorry," I reply, stepping back into the kitchen. "The smell just reminds me of something. Or at least, I think it does." I put my hand over my nose and mouth.

"So, what's your name?"

"Mark," I mutter, "Mark Bliss."

"Hey," she says enthusiastically, "that's my last name, too! My name's Martha Bliss."

Martha… Maggie's granddaughter from my dream. Things are starting to make sense. "What are you doing here? Are you alone?" I ask, remembering that Maggie told me she was beaten to death by a monster, or did she really say eaten to death?

There is a pause, as Martha bangs pots around. "My husband was here too, but he turned a few weeks ago. Truth is, I don't know where he ran off too. When the outbreak happened, this neighborhood was evacuated. We couldn't bear to leave our family home, so we stayed. It's been very quiet, since everyone left. Occasionally, there'll be a crazy outside, but if we're quiet, it'll walk away. Then, we were stormed by a dozen of them. Frank, my husband, held them off, but they got him."

"If you're husband died, then what are you still doing here?" I ask.

"I don't know, really."

I look to my left. Hanging on the wall is a framed photograph. I lean in closer to examine it. I notice it's a Memento Mori photograph, those creep me out more than the living dead. There is a dead, withered, old lady sitting upright on a chair.

"That's my great grandmother, Maggie."

My heart sinks to the floor, as Martha continues.

"Maggie Bliss?" I ask.

"Yeah, that picture was taken back in the eighteen hundreds. She was a big believer in ghosts and talking to spirits. She hosted séances in this house. I know for a fact that she would have loved being alive right now. There's a story that she passed down through generations. We all thought it was silly, but now I'm a believer. She said, that when the dead walk the earth, she will send someone to save the youngest child. They will be the ones to save humanity. I am the youngest child, and you showed up. I guess that's what I'm still doing here, I was waiting for you."

"Yeah maybe," I say, not really sure what to say to something like that. It makes sense, that's why I kept seeing Maggie in my dreams, and why she made me do the things I did to the demented. Not to mention that Maggie first told me that her step grandson died, then in other dreams her granddaughter died. This is just too much to take in.

I continue to stare into the black and white photograph of Maggie. In the background, I hear Martha banging more pots around.

"Thank you for coming, Mark."

As she said that, Maggie's eyes slowly opened revealing that beautiful red color.

EXISTING DEAD

LYLE PEREZ-TINICS

EXISTING DEAD

By Lyle Perez-Tinics
Preview

"Lyle Perez-Tinics takes you on a ride into hell where anything that can go wrong does. *Existing Dead* is a true horror novel that goes for the jugular and even death is not an escape!"

- Edward J. Russell, author of *The Dead Infested*

"Provocative, innovative, and mind numbingly horrific encompass the novel *Existing Dead* by Lyle Perez-Tinics. Unlike any zombie story you've ever read, you'll find yourself immersed in a new vision of terror."

- Nate D. Burleigh, author of *Sustenance*

Prologue

At the moment of birth, life begins to die. But when the rules of life change and death is replaced by an existing hell, the world as we know it ends.

It didn't take the world long to crumble. When the first reports of the dead walking came in, that was it. People began to panic and within an hour of the news broadcast, suicides and murder rates peaked. Some of the population couldn't handle the thought of their lives suddenly changing. The smart folks listened to the National Guard and gathered supplies to wait it out, while the unintelligent thought they could meet the threat head-on. Many small mobs armed themselves with whatever blunt objects they could find. As the dead quickly overran the living, the would-be heroes soon discovered that destroying a human's brain, through the skull, is not as easy as it sounds. Those with firearms lasted a bit longer, but not all of them were marksmen. Once ammunition became a problem, they were massacred. Many reanimated while their intestines were being ripped out of their bellies, and others were eaten whole before they had a chance to reopen their eyes. The dead never stopped looking for victims, they continued on the food's path until they reached it. That is the reason why the dead outnumbered the living ten to one.

Kyle Reynolds was in the smarter group.

Kyle, a thirty-five year old welder from Nevada, formerly from sunny Southern California, was nothing more than that. He had married a woman who was not the one meant for him, and they had a son together. The boy's name was Eddie and they loved him. Kyle and his wife, Mary, were constantly fighting. If it wasn't one reason, it was another. When the dead began attacking the living, things didn't change between them. Instead of fighting about sex and money, they fought about supplies and safety.

The three of them took refuge in the basement of their Nevada home. They were only down there for a few days, but that was long enough for Kyle's hatred toward Mary to intensify. He was only there to protect his son and nothing more. To help give him some extra time, he would have been more than happy to throw Mary into a horde of hungry monsters. But the chances of the dead finding a way in were low. The basement doors were reinforced with steel beams that Kyle had welded shut. The only way out was through a small tunnel that led up to the front yard. His thinking was that if anything began banging on the doors, there would be another way out. Supplies of water, canned food, and entertainment were stacked to the roof.

Eddie's safety was not the only thing he was worried about. There was something else on his mind, something that made his heart ache. In a secret compartment in his wallet, he carried an old, creased photo of a woman. From time to time, he would take the picture out and stare at it. He had never been able to let Jasmine go and always wondered what life would have been like if he had married her. Jasmine was Kyle's *real* love, and he wished that things in his life could have been different. Gazing at the picture, something inside his heart told him that he had to go and find her. He had to make sure that she was okay, and if she wasn't, then he would make her safe, like he'd done with Eddie and Mary. There was only one thing holding Kyle back.

As Kyle sat on a chair in the corner looking at the old picture of Jasmine, he felt eyes on him. He glanced up and staring at him was the worried gaze of Eddie. Kyle smiled devilishly in hopes of getting a reaction from his son. The little boy was only eight-years-old; he didn't fully understand what was going on and why he couldn't go outside to play with Gary, the next-door neighbor's kid. It hurt Kyle to think what was really going on in his son's mind. Was he hurt? Confused? Sad? Depressed? Did he find Kyle's devilish grin funny? But there was no reaction; Eddie continued to stare at him with those eyes that always tore Kyle into pieces. He looked down at the picture of Jasmine again, her bright blue eyes seemed to smile back at him, calling him, begging him for help. A thought of him running his hand through her soft blond hair ran through his mind. The fantasy quickly turned to horror as that same memory was replaced with an image of a dead hand ripping her hair out and biting into her face. It was then that Kyle realized he would have to make the toughest decision of his life.

Chapter One

"So what? You're just gonna leave us?" Mary demanded an answer with her hands on her hips. Her hazel eyes stared at him like a vulture stalking its prey. Her long black hair fell down toward her face. The shine of her hair made her eyes glow.

"I'll only be gone for a few days. I'll be back; there's just something that I have to do," Kyle replied as he stuffed more things into Eddie's robot themed knapsack.

"Are you going to take my backpack, Daddy?" Eddie asked from behind them, Kyle turned just in time to see Eddie's eyes water.

"I am, Sport, is that okay? I can look for something else if you want me to. I thought you would be okay with me taking this. Y'know, so I can have something of yours to keep near me," Kyle said as he reached into his pocket. "I'll tell you what, let me hold on to your backpack and I'll let you hold on to my lucky four leaf-clover keychain."

"Really?" Eddie asked with delight. Even though it was just a fake four-leaf clover encased in plastic, he loved it.

"Yeah, really." Kyle took the keychain off the metal ring and placed it in Eddie's cupped hand. The boy closed his hand and put the four-leaf clover in his pocket. Kyle stared back at the small table where he continued packing a few bags of chips and some bottles of water.

"So what are you gonna go do?" Mary asked.

"Nothing that concerns you," Kyle snapped. He wasn't in the mood to be asked a million questions. There was nothing that he could say that would get Mary off his back.

"Well, if it's something that's going to make you leave your son, then, yes, it does."

"I'm glad you said it like that because if it was just you and me in here, I would have left your ass a long time ago. I probably wouldn't even have let you in here. I would have left you outside so *they*, the disgusting freaks outside, could get you," Kyle said, not really realizing the impact that those comments would make on Eddie.

And as if on cue, Eddie spoke up, "You're not going to protect Mommy from the bad people anymore?"

"I didn't mean that, Eddie."

"Well, what did you mean, Kyle?" Mary responded. Her eyes turned red with anger. The vein that always appeared on her forehead when she was mad began to make an entrance.

Kyle felt trapped. He was being cornered by his wife and son. "Why don't you go put on your headphones and play your video game, okay, Sport?" Kyle said.

"Sure, Dad," Eddie replied and walked to his chair. The handheld video console and headphones were on a countertop next to the chair. He grabbed the earphones and put them on.

As soon as he saw Eddie playing his game happily, Kyle continued, "You know what I meant, Mary. Face it, I don't love you, and I know for a fact that you don't love me. The only reason we're together is because of Eddie." He stuffed a change of clothes into the backpack. "If he wasn't here, we would have gone our separate ways a long time ago."

"So is that what you want now? To go our separate ways? Jesus fucking Christ, Kyle. We're in the middle of the fucking apocalypse and you're letting our issues get in the way."

"Well, maybe I have to. The world looks like it's ending so this is my only chance."

"You're only chance to do what? What is it that's so important that you would leave your son and me behind?"

"We already went over this, Mary. I wanted to leave you a long time ago, but Eddie always made me stay. I never got the chance to tell you, but I filed for divorce a day before the dead started coming back to life." Mary was about to interrupt, but Kyle kept going. "I was going to tell you the next day, but I had to start worrying about protecting Eddie. I did what I said I was going to do. He's safe down here. No one is getting in. Those metal doors are welded shut and the only way out is through the vent I dug. Both of you will be safe here. I'll only be gone a few days, maybe a little more." He paused for a moment.

"You filed for divorce?" was all she said, cold and stern.

"I just told you I did," he replied.

"Where's the paperwork? I wanna make this easier for you to leave."

Kyle turned and walked to a small work desk. He opened a drawer and took out a manila folder. He walked back to Mary. "Here," he said and tossed the folder onto the table.

"I'm going to tell you this right now, Kyle," she said searching for a pen. "If I sign these papers, I'm never going to let you see Eddie again when the world goes back to normal. He doesn't need a father who's going to leave him behind for no reason."

"If you try to keep him from me, then I'll take you to court and we'll let a judge decide who gets him. But keep in mind, Mary, I'm not the one with a drug history, I'm not the one with a criminal background, I'm not the one without a job, and I'm not the one threatening you with Eddie!" Kyle stuffed the last of his supplies into the backpack. "I should have never left Jasmine when I found out that you were pregnant," Kyle added, instantly regretting mentioning Jasmine in the conversation.

"Jasmine? Who the hell is Jasmine?" Mary's eyes half closed.

"She's no one, just a girl from my past."

"Who the fuck is she?" Mary screamed. Kyle could see the crazed expression on her face. Her eyes continued to glow with anger and disgust, along with that, her complexion began to redden.

"Jasmine is the girl I left because of you!" Kyle screamed. "We were perfectly happy together until you told me you were pregnant."

"So you were fucking someone after we broke up?"

"You were the one who broke up with me!" Kyle raised his voice louder. He noticed that Eddie looked up from his game. They both stared at their child as he looked back down at his distraction. "You were the one who said you didn't love me anymore and that I was better off with someone else. After hearing that for years, I finally started realizing that you were right. I *was* better off with someone else. And when I was, you couldn't handle that. You kept blowing up my cell phone when me and Jasmine were on dates. You kept leaving me messages of you blubbering, saying you wanted me back. I fell for that so many times, but not anymore! I was finally happy with Jasmine and you fucked that up when you told me you were pregnant!"

Mary started crying. "Fuck you," she said slowly and softly. "Is that who you're running off to be with? Jasmine? She's the one who's making you turn your back on me and Eddie?"

"No, Mary. You're the one who made me turn my back on *you*. The only reason I came back to you was for Eddie. I thought I could love you again, but I quickly realized that I couldn't. You're not the one I want to be with. I have to go see if Jasmine is safe. You and Eddie can stay here till this blows over. I'll more than likely be back before then. If I can, I'll bring Jasmine with me so we can all wait this out. You can take me to court for Eddie when everything goes back to normal, but I'm more stable than you. You won't be able to keep him from me."

Neither one of them truly believed that the world would be able to recover from something like this. It was more of a comforting thought of hope, something to keep them going, a light at the end of their dark tunnel. But neither of them wanted to take the chance that if things *did* go back to normal, they'd each know what they wanted. They didn't want to be together anymore, and signing divorce papers was a start.

Mary opened the manila folder. She quickly found where she needed to sign and gave it a quick signature. Kyle's was already there. Mary closed the folder and threw it to Kyle. He clumsily caught the envelope and stuffed it in the backpack. Kyle knew that just because the papers were signed, it didn't mean much. Getting divorced was never this easy.

"Now we're divorced, go do whatever the fuck you want to. But listen to what I'm going to tell you. If you leave, you'll never see me and Eddie again," Mary said.

"Whatever. That's the difference between you and me. If this was reversed I'd never keep Eddie away from you."

"Well I guess that makes you a better person than me, huh?" Mary said matter-of-factly.

Kyle turned and walked to his gun rack. There were only three guns, but he had an abundance of ammo for each one. First, he grabbed his Glock 24 and a box of cartridges. He loaded all the magazines he had for it, five in total, and put them in the side pockets of the robot backpack. He grabbed the holster for the handgun and put it around his waist, then holstered the firearm. Next he grabbed the .357 Magnum Revolver. He grabbed a box of rounds and began loading the cylinder. He put the .357 on the countertop next to the backpack. He turned to the gun rack and grabbed the Winchester 1300 Tactical shotgun by the pistol grip. The gun was fully equipped with a stock and pistol grip for shooting preferences. Kyle grabbed the box of ammo next to it and loaded eight shells into the shotgun. He tossed the rest of the shells in the backpack. By now the pack was filled to the top with supplies. He had problems zipping it up, but, when he finally got the rucksack to zip, he loosened one of the straps and flung it over his shoulder. It felt awkward on his back, but he had no other options.

Kyle grabbed the .357 with some extra rounds and walked over to Mary, who had taken a seat next to Eddie. He handed the gun to her and said, "Here, take this, just in case something tries to get in." Mary took the gun and the box of ammunition. "It's loaded, be careful with this one. It's very powerful. Keep Eddie safe."

Kyle poked Eddie on the top of the head. The boy took off his headphones and looked at his dad. "I'm going to go out for a few days okay, Sport?"

Okay, Dad," he said as he put his earbuds back on.

"That's all I'm going to get? Can I have a hug?" Kyle asked not really expecting an answer.

"Just leave him alone, Kyle. He's angry that you're leaving him." Mary began to rub Eddie's back. "Just fucking leave already," she said softly, her voice trailing into her sorrows.

"I'll be back, Sport, okay? I'll make sure to bring back a lot of games for your handheld," Kyle said. Eddie nodded in return. "I love you, buddy," he continued then turned toward the little window near the vent.

He grabbed the shotgun off the table as he walked to the vent. The world around him began to move in slow motion as he leaned the shotgun on the wall and lifted the vent door. He put the backpack and shotgun through the slot, and then climbed in. There was only enough room for him to crawl toward the opening in the front yard. He moved forward, pushing the pack and shotgun in front of him. The vent began to widen. There was more room for him to move. He saw a little patch of sunlight hitting the inside of the vent, but wasn't entirely sure what to expect with the light at the end of the tunnel.

Kyle made it to the light and there was enough room for him to stand. He hunched over so the top of his head wouldn't hit the metal entrance. He lifted the door slowly and poked his head out. He searched the area for movement. There was none. Grabbing the backpack and the shotgun, he placed them on the grass and climbed out, closing the hatch door behind him. Movement was everything now. Making less noise would ensure the he wouldn't bring on unnecessary attention. He picked up the pack and the shotgun from the dew-filled grass and stood.

He searched the area again as he lifted the shotgun in a shooting stance. His blue 1995 Toyota pickup truck was still sitting on the driveway untouched. Kyle walked toward the vehicle, but suddenly stopped. He knew that he was about to do something stupid and dangerous. All he wanted was to get one last look at Eddie before he left.

Kyle casually walked toward the very small basement window. It was only one foot across and six inches high, Kyle never understood the reason for such a small window. Laying the weapon and backpack on the ground, he lay on the grass and peered through. The window was covered with a thick layer of moisture. He wiped his hand across the window a few times to clear it. He peered in again to get a glimpse of his boy. Mary stood behind Eddie's chair with the .357 drawn and pointed at the back of his head. Eddie continued playing his video game as if nothing was wrong. She pulled the hammer back on the gun.

"No!" Kyle yelled as loud as he could. His heart sank and his body felt completely numb.

The scream was loud enough for Eddie to hear through the headphones. The little boy looked up at his dad and gave a quick smile. Kyle noticed that Eddie had the four-leaf clover keychain dangling around his finger.

At that second, Mary pulled the trigger. Kyle watched, in slow motion, as the bullet ejected from the gun and went through the back of the boy's head. It exploded outward, leaving a large hole where Eddie's face had been. Blood, cartilage, brain tissue, and other unknown substances spewed everywhere onto the ground. His bottom jaw was still intact, but the top of his mouth was mixed with the gore on the floor. Eddie dropped the handheld as he went limp. His arms fell down the sides of the couch. The keychain fell out of his finger and hit the ground.

"No!" Kyle screeched again even louder than before. He began to weep uncontrollably at the sight.

Mary stared at the glass window. She shouted something, but he couldn't hear it over his mourning. Through tears, Kyle watched as Mary put the gun barrel under her chin and pulled the trigger. A look of disbelief crossed Mary's face as the bullet went through her head, leaving a baseball-sized hole as blood and brain ejected across the room. She instantly fell to the ground and dropped the firearm a foot away from her hand.

Kyle was sick to his stomach and he began to vomit, showering the little window with his digested breakfast. He quickly backed away from the acrid mess. His eyes watered and tears began to fall freely down his face. Everything around him seemed to slow to a crawl, his senses heightened as adrenalin pumped through his veins. His hearing increased for a split second. He could hear each individual bird chirp and then he heard a moan from somewhere in the area. He wiped away his tears and quickly heaved to his feet, picking up the weapon and his supplies. Kyle still felt hollow inside, but his survival instincts kicked in, even though mentally, he wasn't there.

Five bodies walked toward him. Their skins were grayish green and their clothes were shredded over their forms. The walking corpses were thin; their exposed skin looked to be stretched over bones. They walked slowly, carefully taking one step at a time. He needed to get past them in order to make it to his truck. Kyle raised the Winchester and fired. The shell caught the front monster in the chest, nearly splitting it in half. The creature fell back as Kyle pumped the shotgun. He aimed at another and fired again. The casing hit it in the head; the force of the slug causing its head to explode, expelling brain matter and bone fragments in a burst pattern.

Kyle kept repeating the words, "I'm sorry, Eddie," as he shot off the remaining shells. He began moving toward the truck gripping the gun like a baseball bat, ready to swing at anything that might creep up behind him. He tossed the shotgun into the vehicle, and then threw the bag in. Another moan erupted. Kyle quickly drew his pistol like an old west gunfighter and turned. Standing before him was Gary, Eddie's friend, wearing a gray hooded sweater and a vacant look on his face. His black Beatles-type hair was wild and unkempt. Kyle pointed the gun at the boy's head, but couldn't pull the trigger. The creature's eyes widened and his mouth dropped open as he lunged for Kyle. Kyle quickly put the handgun down and kicked the boy across the chest. Gary moaned as the force of Kyle's kick caused the reanimated kid to fall to the ground, but as he hit the grass, he was already trying to get back to his feet. Kyle jumped into the truck and started it. He closed the door and simultaneously, Gary's face pressed up against the window. Kyle motioned away from the glass in shock. The boy continued hitting the door with his palm.

The momentary safety of the truck caused Kyle to fall into a trance. He sat in the driver seat repeating, "I'm sorry, Eddie." He grabbed the shotgun sitting next to him and put the barrel under his chin. "I'm sorry, Eddie," he mumbled, and pulled the trigger.

The shotgun clicked empty, and when it did something clicked in Kyle's head. The hollowness was still inside of him, but he began to think clearly. He turned to look at Gary again. "I'm sorry, Gary," he said and put the shotgun on the passenger seat.

Kyle put the truck into reverse and backed out of the driveway. He shifted into drive and headed west up

Colonial Road. He glanced through his rearview mirror and saw the figure of Gary walking onto the street, lumbering in his direction.

Buy the complete book at **www.ExistingDead.com**
or at www.Amazon.com

Available in print and eBook.

About the Author

Lyle Perez-Tinics (Writer/Editor/Publisher) is the creator of **Undead in the Head Reviews** (www.UndeadintheHead.com) a website dedicated to zombie books and the authors. He is the owner & Editor-in-Chief of **Rainstorm Press** (wwwRainstormPress.com) and owner of **The Mad Formatter** (www.TheMadFormatter.com) a book interior design business. He has stories in many anthologies and is currently promoting his zombie novel *Existing Dead*. He is the mastermind behind The Undead That Saved Christmas charity anthology series.

Twitter - @LylePerez @RainstormPress @UndeadintheHead

www.Facebook.com/RainstormPress

www.Facebook.com/UndeadintheHead

To read more about his work, please visit his website.

www.ExistingDead.com

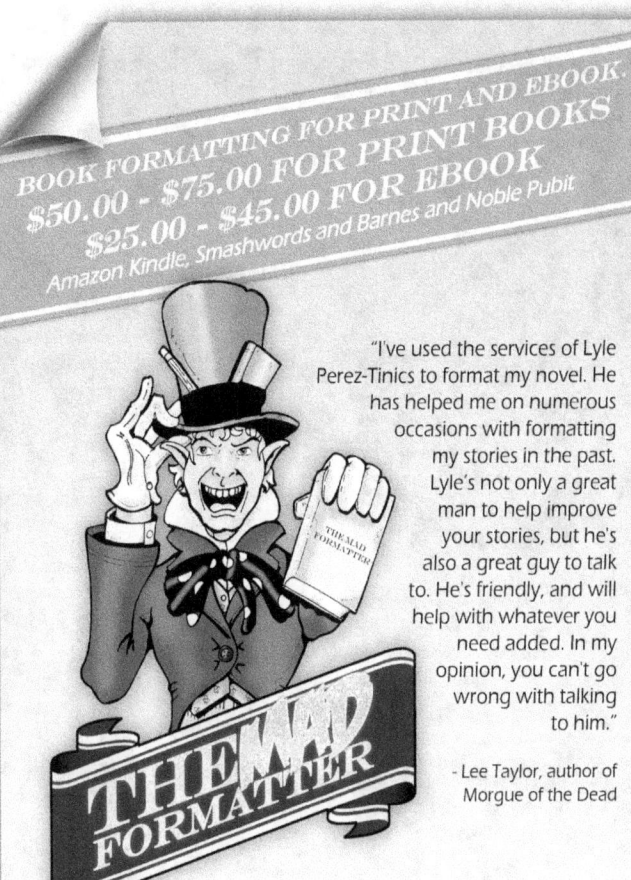

Welcome to *Z Magazine...*

The first magazine written by zombies for zombies

"Being undead isn't easy and never has been.

We die and come back. Whether because of viruses, voodoo, or unknown causes, the result is always the same. The living question the purpose of their existence all the time and rarely come up with definitive answers, but when zombies ask themselves that question it's even harder to answer.

Z Magazine is here to change the way media treats the undead. We're here to help you embrace the perfect, rotting corpse that you are. Our mission is to give you hope that zombies are making progress in this world. There are models, designers, chefs, parents, and other real people out there who are proud to say they are the walking dead."

Z Magazine is a full color magazine printed on heavyweight paper. It contains satirical, humorous, and thoughtful articles written from the perspective of zombies living in a reality where humans and the undead cohabitate. There are advertisements for shows and products catered to the undead as well as photography and illustrations of zombies.

www.thezombiemag.com